Love Breaks my Bones, And I Laugh

stories by
Couri Johnson

Published by Pumpernickel House
an imprint of Pumpernickel House Publishing
New Orleans, LA. USA.

Edited by Jason Bargueno and Couri Johnson
Cover Art by Couri Johnson

p h

"Clown Town" originally appeared in *Thrice Fiction*
"Little Things" originally appeared in *Enizagam*

Love Breaks My Bones and I Laugh

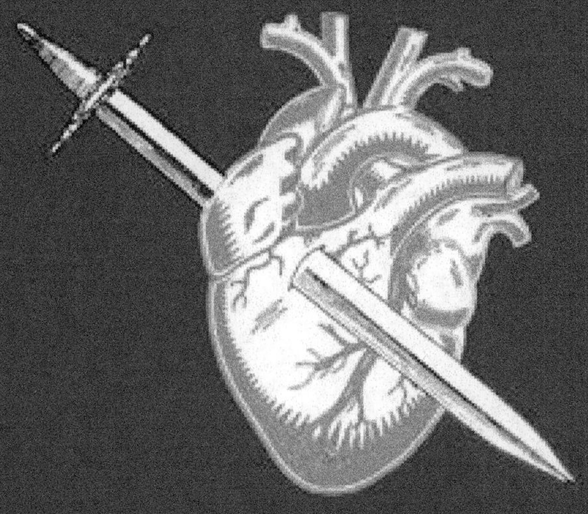

stories by
Couri Johnson

To Devin and Reid,
and all the other men
who never loved me.

Contents

Possible Dedications for My Next Short Story Collection

1.
To my mother, who always paid attention to me. Who conditioned me to believe that everyone would and should want to pay attention to me. Who told me I was special, every day, forcibly, at every turn, for little things like getting jam smeared around my mouth and leaving it there for hours even though I neurotically needed to wash my hands every thirty minutes or so. My mother, who loved me so much before she died that she convinced me the rest of the world would love me too, always, and so I used to trust everyone, to look everyone in the eye, to go to everyone with open arms. To my mother, god damn you, are you proud of what you've done?

2.
To my ex-fiancé
Who said loving me was like running a half-marathon.
Yes, it was exhilarating, yes, it was exciting, yes, it felt like an accomplishment doing it, but it was also exhausting, and it was also difficult, and it was also painful, and eventually you'd come to a point where you'd end up wondering why, exactly, you were putting yourself through all this.

3.
To that perfect day I spent on the beach of Shodoshima
Where I came to love boat trips. I love the way there is nothing
but wind and water and the rest of the world is just a silhouette
behind a hazy sheet of air. The sound of the horn and the motor
and the ship cutting through the waves. The constant rocking
feeling—like you are a small thing in the arms of someone that
loves you, like you are being cared for and put to sleep. I loved
the feeling of the rail in my hands, and his hands on my hips,
as the island came into view; first just one big grey hump of a
thing, like a great beast rising out of the sea, before distance
allowed its details to come into view; the houses on the hill,
the winding roads like serpents, and the old man on the dock,
pausing his fishing to wave as we drew near.
And most of all, I love how ghosts can't cross the salty sea. They
have to wait on the opposite shore for you to return.

4.
To my childhood dog.
I know you're dead and even if you weren't dead, you couldn't
read. At least I don't think you could read. Sometimes though
I would watch you laying on the floor with your head turned
towards the bookshelf, and you would stay that way for so long,
a glazed look in your eyes as they flitted up and down the book
spines, and I'd wonder what you were doing, what you were
thinking about. Maybe, just maybe, you were making sense out
of the letters, stringing them together into words. Maybe you
knew more than you let on. Maybe that's why you chewed up
the journal where I said your head was too big for your body
and your breath smelled like old man's underwear. I'm sorry
about that, okay, but it was true. That doesn't mean I didn't love
you, though. I did love you. I do. I still do.

5.

To my former counselor,
Who needs to learn how to better regulate their emotional
responses now, bitch?

6.

To myself,
Party in the streets, real anxious in the sheets.

7.

To my ex fiancé
See, I don't need you, I am strong and independent and success-
ful, and who are you? No, really? Who are you? You aren't the
person I fell in love with. Nevermind, don't bother answering
that. I don't care. Besides, I already met someone new.

8.

To the girl I met at the playground two weeks ago,
Hey, I don't know if maybe I got your number wrong or something, but you seemed really cool and I was just wondering,
like, if it would be cool to meet for coffee, like I mean I know
life must busy and all since you can't seem to text back, but I
just think it could be cool, I mean, hey who knows you know?
Haha, smiley face. Anyway, you have my contact information,
hit me up.

9.

To my childhood dog,
I even loved the way you ate everything. Trash, books, and even
my clothes. But only my clothes. My mother said it was because
you wanted to protect me from other predators by getting rid of
my smell. But I think it was because you were hungry. Hungry
for nearness. Because you're the closest thing I'll ever have to a
child of my own in this life, so it would make sense for us to be
alike. And I? I know that hunger well.

10.
To the cockroach who hid itself in the toilet paper in my old apartment, and sprung out to land on my bare thigh
We had some disagreements, you and I, and we fought a long war. You were a worthy adversary. And I am sorry. I am sorry that I killed you. I am sorry you are dead because of me. I am sorry that because I could not understand you and you could not understand me it had to come to war at all. I would have liked it better if I could have put you outside, if you could have gone on living, but sometimes that's just not an option. Sometimes, death has to happen. When there is a war, there must be a victor. When there is a war, there has to be death. I don't make up these rules, I just live by them.

11.
To my ex fiancé
You were wrong about me,
I'm not a half marathon.
I'm a whole ass fucking marathon, baby, and it's not my fault you were too much of a weakling to stick it out.

12.
To my ex-fiancé
I'm sorry, baby, I didn't mean what I said. I still love you, I'll always love you. Please come back, baby, we can work it out.

13.
To my mother;
Who didn't want to tell me dragons didn't actually exist, who didn't want to tell me anything that could hurt. So I went out into the world thinking the world would do me the same courtesy, that the world would be kind and only tell me kind things, and yes, that was decidedly a mistake.

14.
To that perfect day I spent on the beach of Shodoshima,
When I ate ice cream and let it dry in a sticky sweet ring around
my mouth and every time he kissed me he tasted that sugar and
he would smile.

15.
To my childhood dog,
Because you loved me more than anything else ever will, even
though I said you had a big dumb head and stanky breath. Even
though I've got a big dumb head and stanky breath.

16.
To my former counselor,
All of the books you suggested I read talked about practicing
secure attachments. In fact, all of the books you suggested suggested to me that it was completely okay to practice secure attachments with a licensed counselor or therapist. That a secure
attachment to a licensed counselor or therapist was completely
valid, even if you were paying them for it. That your counselor
and or therapist can be your primary attachment and that is
perfectly ok, maybe even great. These books, they said it a lot,
and I mean, we did text every day. I guess, what I'm saying here,
is if you wanted to be with me you could have just told me so,
you didn't need to make me read all these books. Haha smiley
face. You are going to have to leave your husband though, I
won't be anyone's side piece.

17
To myself,
Because no one else deserves me.

18.
To myself
Because no one else will have me.

19.
To my ex fiancé
Come on, baby. Baby, come on.

20.
To that perfect day I spent on the beach of Shodoshima,
There is an inlet there called the angel road. It's a narrow strip
of sand connecting a small wooded isle to the main island, and
when the tide rushes in, it disappears, and when the tide rushes
out it's exposed, and people come from all around to see it do
this dance. To hide, then to reveal, and then hide again. Such a
flirt, that sandbar. Such a little tease. And yet so beloved. And
maybe I am hoping to do the same thing. Maybe I am hoping
people will love me the same for the way I reveal myself, and for
how afterwards, I always run away.

21.
To my ex fiancé,
(Heavy breathing, wide eyed stare.)

22.
To my mother,
Because I became a writer for you. Because I wanted to bring
you back to life somehow. Because I wanted to give you some
kind of immortality. Because I thought you could maybe breath
again through words and paper. Because everything I do is con-
nected to you, somehow, and your death—from the way that
I speak to the way that I laugh to the way that my hands move
and the way that I take my coffee to the way that I love cheap
diners and the woods and the smell of mud to the way that I am
lonely to the way that I want to be alone to the way that I am
always wary to the way that I never want anyone to leave to the
way that I trust too much to the way I am always trying to fall
in love. I am your mirror; this book is an altar I have built for
you, the grave you never got. Everything I do, mother, is a re-

flection of you. Except maybe when I use the bathroom. Maybe that I do just cause I have to.

23.

To my former counselor.

I'm sorry, baby, I didn't mean what I said. I still love you, I'll always love you. Please come back, baby, we can work it out.

24.

To the cockroach I murdered in cold blood for coming into my apartment, even though he couldn't know, no, that he was doing something wrong, even though he couldn't know, no, what was happening to him, why his body hurt so much, why the air suddenly tasted so wrong, and he had tried to run yes he had tried to run and I kept spraying, I kept spraying while he laid there twitching because in war there has to be death because he had touched me because I hadn't wanted to be touched but he couldn't have known that, no, he couldn't have known anything at all and so maybe there was no war, maybe I am just a killer, yes, maybe I am just cruel

I'm sorry, okay, I'm sorry.

25.

To my ancestors,

Who I've heard supposedly were great. Who I've heard, supposedly, were aristocrats, warriors, poets, people of status and wealth. Explorers, and seekers, setting out to take the wild world in their own hands. I often wonder if they're watching me now. If they are, I want them to consider the steps they took that lead our blood here; the choices they made that burdened me to exist. I want them to watch, and I want them to rue their mistakes.

26.
To my childhood dog
To my mother
To the cockroach
Things have to die, you know, they die, and that's all there is to
it. We all die. I will die eventually too, okay, and be with you
then, I promise. Everyone is going to die, and there's nothing I
can do about it and there is nothing more I can do for you other
than write this, okay? So please, please, please, stop haunting
me.

28.
To my former counselor
(Wide eyed stare, heavy breathing.)

29.
To the girl I met on the playground
U up? Haha smiley face

30.
To that perfect day on the beach on shodoshima,
I had eaten icecream and sat in the sand with my exfiance, and
we had watched as the tide came in and we had watched as the
tide went out, hand in hand, and the sun baked into our skin.
The next day we'd be burnt and we'd peel for weeks after and
touching each other would hurt. It would hurt too much to
touch. But that day, there was no pain. We watched angel road
reveal itself as the tide rolled back, and we stood on the shore
and we skipped stones, and he kissed me, and it wasn't like running, it was like sugar; all sticky sweetness. And I looked down
into the water, and I looked up into his eyes, and I thought I
could pull my own tide back, that I could part my waters and
show him what was resting on my ocean floor, and there would
be no need to run, after, there would be no need to bury it again
in the sand. Because this was before, of course, that perfect day

on Shodoshima was before it all, and nothing hurt. There were no ghosts following us. There was no effort to our love, no blood on our hands. But we stayed too long out in the sun, you know, and the next day our skin was so red, as if someone had slapped us hard all over trying to wake us up. But that perfect day on Shodoshima was before, you know, just before it hurt too much to touch.

A Shard

If I could go back to the first night we met, I would tell you
the story of the Snow Queen. The Snow Queen really isn't the
villain of the story, you know. It is someone else entirely. It is
something else entirely. The whole problem is really one pin-
prick of glass so small you can hardly see it with your eye. If I
could go back and tell you anything it would be that—that the
things that hurt most are sometimes the least noticeable.
Or maybe I'd go back and decide never to meet you at all, but
we both know that's not true, nor even if it were possible, actually possible.

No, I would go back. I would meet you all over again,
and this would be what I would actually tell you.

I have a bad habit of not being loved. It wasn't always like that, I
think, when I was younger it was not so much like that. At least.
I remember my mother once loving me dearly. But in all stories,
mother's die, and this story is no different than those. Regardless, when I first noticed this habit, I was just a small thing,
shabby and sixteen with new breasts and a new habit of following this boy who I thought might love me. Once I followed him
into the woods, where and when we were not supposed to be,
where everyone dumped their trash. We we're picking through

it—finding this scrap of metal or this copper wire that he would deposit in his car which he left nearby on the side of the road. And then finally he picked me up and he laid me down on the ground among the trash and took me.

While he did, I reached out my arm—flung it out—is the word, I guess—and something pricked me so sharp and deep when we left, all the fallen leaves that'd been bellow my hand had filled up like little cups with my blood. Maybe I hadn't cried out, or maybe I had, and he'd taken it wrong, or maybe he hadn't cared that I'd been hurt. Because you see, that's when I think it happened. That something got inside of me that made it a habit of sorts for people to never love me. Right after, his face had gotten so ugly over mine, and then after, he never did treat me the same even if he still took me every now and then. It was never a love thing, is what I am saying. I have never been really, truly loved.

And it's all because that prick—I'm thinking now it must have been a shard of glass you see. A very special and small shard.

Here is how The Snow Queen starts. People, adaptations, they are always forgetting this. They probably think it is too strange, or don't see the meaning behind it. But I know Hans. I know Hans like the back of my hand. Hans and I suffer from the same affliction, you see. That little shard. That invisible prick.

No one ever loved Hans either. At least not when he was alive. At least not in the way that he needed and wanted so very desperately.

Anyway, there is a devil with a mirror, and he is the beginning of it all. A mirror that distorts everything and makes everything ugly so you can't see the beauty in it. He and his devil friends are going to use it to play a nasty trick in heaven. But it breaks on the way and the pieces scatter everywhere and get in people's eyes and hearts. Now, Hans says that when this happens it makes it impossible for them to see the beauty in anything, and maybe for those with it in their eyes that's true.

But mine is in my heart, and I still see so much beauty. Beauty in you, and in all the other's I've followed behind asking please, please, the way Hans used to.

Do you remember the first night we met? Do you remember the nights after? Do you spend any time at all thinking of them the way I do?

There are some nights when the world is all light and beauty, and I feel very nearly loved. The streetlights seem like moons and suns and the glass shards in the road whole galaxies sparkling under their light, and the hand in my hand something permanent and steady and kind. It's a rare feeling and when it happens it feels so good that my heart might nearly split in two. What would happen then? Would the shard release and flow back out of my blood stream? Could I cough it up and finally be free?

I think love could do that.

I thought you might love me, that first night. I thought you could grow to, steady and strong like a tree, and then maybe I could shake free the shard, and have a safe place to rest where someone finally thinks I am beautiful.

There were moments, weren't there? Where you very nearly said I was beautiful. I could see you look at me and your mouth would purse like something was waiting there behind it, hanging off of your tongue. What was there?

You never told me. Instead, like all the others, you started to run.

I have figured out something Hans was wrong about. You see the shards in the eyes, the shards in the heart, they're different. They have to be different. The shards in the eyes, yes, they make you see things as ugly and distorted, and for a long time I thought maybe I was always chasing after people like that, like Hans must have thought, too.

But it's too many. No mirror can be that big. There can't be that many shards. And you—I've seen you see beauty in so many things. So many things that weren't me. It was you and your love of all things that weren't me that started me asking: "What is it that is wrong with me?"

That made me remember the prick and the shard that started it all, the leaves like cups of blood, and how many men have turned away and turned away and turned away, despite me reaching with my pricked hand and asking please.

But I have it figured out now. Those with shards in their heart, they don't see the world as ugly and distorted. How can they? The shard isn't anywhere they can see. Instead, people look at them, look into them, and they see the shard. They see the ugliness and the distortion, the no-goodness of it all--they see it in us. In people like me and Hans. They see it, and they know we are sick, and they run.

Didn't you say something like that to me once—that there was something inside of me that made me hard to love?

There is a boy and there is a girl in the Snow Queen. They are who the story is about. The Snow Queen, she is just a set piece. She is just someone who is there. Kai and Gerda, this is who the story is about. And they love each other, until Kai no longer loves Gerda. It's all because of the mirror, you see, in Kai's eye. He runs from her to the Snow Queen. And she follows.

Because Gerda is Hans, Gerda is me, always following

after love even if it takes us to the coldest places. Or at least that is what I thought before you.

Gerda, though, she has no shard in her heart. People love Gerda along the way. They help her. And she is able, because of that, to get to the coldest place. To get to The Snow Queen's castle. The Snow Queen, who wants to keep Kai despite his coldness. Despite his lack of love. Because no one loves the Snow Queen.

She, everyone thinks, is some kind of monster. But all she ever really wanted was someone there. Someone to give her the word eternity despite being surrounded by nothing but ice.

See, I know now I was wrong. Hans and I aren't Gerda. It is the Snow Queen, like us, that had a shard of the Devil's Mirror in her heart.

She ends up alone at the end of it all.

Do you remember the last time you very nearly called me beautiful? When we were walking together down the lamp-lit street and all the broken bottles were sparkling like something promising rather than something hurtful? You had swung me around as we walked down the road against your chest, and there I could hear the beat of your unpricked heart, and I thought that beat was for me.

It was a beautiful thing to think.

And I told you then that I love you.

And your arms fell from around my waist and you stepped away to look at me—to really look at me, and your lips pursed, like you were going to say that thing that had been waiting behind them for so long—that thing I had been waiting for since I'd been pricked—and you said:

"I'm sorry."

In the end, it is Gerda's love that saves Kai from the shard in his eye. She loves him so hard he cries it all out. But I cannot seem to cry out the shard in my heart, and I cannot find anyone to love away the sickness if the sickness is that I am unlovable. I have thought hard about this. I thought hard about it as you walked away that night, leaving me among the glass shards on the ground and the cheap streetlights that had blotted out all the stars.

I sat thinking there for a long time on the curb, and walking the street looking at the shards. One of them, I thought, must be the key. A part of the mirror. The mirror that makes it all so ugly and distorted.

I thought how the worst thing in the world was to see love and beauty when no one could see it in you.

I thought about the Snow Queen, alone in her castle, asking for eternity with no one coming to save her, to cry over her, to dislodge the shard in her heart. How tiresome it gets, being seen by the world one way when you can only see the love that you can't receive.

And so, you see, that is why I did it.

If I could go back to that first night when you very nearly may have loved me, I would have told you all this. I would have told you that I needed you to cut me open with love and to extract the shard in my heart before you said goodbye. I would have asked you to close your eyes and say that I am beautiful and that you loved me, even if you didn't mean it, because that, I think, would have pulled the shard out and made it possible for you to mean it. And I think you, above all people, who can see such beauty in the world, could have done it. But you didn't, and now it's all lost.

I would have told you what was at stake—perhaps I

didn't know exactly then, but it was growing, of course, in my mind. These things grow, sturdy and slow, and take over. A weed of a thought.

That this was the last time I could do this. Before I would have to try something else.

But I didn't. And you left me alone on the street with the glass and all the hurtful things.

And so I sat there, all night alone, shifting through them, looking through them, pricking my palms and watering the cement with rivulets of my blood. It's hard to know which piece, of course, is a shard of the mirror, which will relieve me of my want for love.

So, in the end, I just started pressing them all to my eyes and seeing which would stick.

I didn't come here to make you feel bad. I did not follow you here to try and earn your love. That is over now. I only wanted to show you my eyes.

You see they are different now. The way I see is different now. You do not have to worry about hurting me, about me loving you too much when you cannot love me back. You do not have to worry about that at all anymore. The glass is just glass, the streetlights just streetlights, and you just a person, ugly and small like all other persons who see me as ugly and small. I have fixed it—what drove you away, I have fixed it. I see the world entirely rationally now.

So you can stay, if you want. You could stay.

Ma

He had won her the hermit crab at a local church festival he'd gone to. She didn't want it. It reminded her of a hard, orange spider, and the click of its legs against the small plastic bottom made her skin crawl. He handed it to her when she met him at the door. She said thank you and put it on her windowsill.

"Do you think you'll be ready to go back to work soon?" He asked.

"It's only been a week." She hunched her shoulders as he ran his hands over her arms and looked to the window where the crab was. "I keep wondering if they know."

"Even if they did, they wouldn't care." He guided her to sit down on the bed. "What are you going to name it?"

"I don't know," she said.
When they laid down together, she could hear it shuffling from side to side. She could see the outline of its bulb eyes. He pushed his hand up her skirt, and she felt his fingernails scrape her thigh. She closed her eyes and pinched the tip of her tongue between her teeth and thought about the words "this time."
At the end of the night, she wrapped her blanket around her shoulders and watched him disappear down the street. Eventually all that was left for her to see was the crab, and the curve of its claw pointing towards the streetlamp. It pinched closed on nothing. She imagined slipping her finger between it. If it would hurt.

She laid down and listened to the crab clack across the cage. It was too small, she thought. Maybe she should buy it a new one. Three days later the crab was dead.

"Did you remember to feed it?" He was holding the container in his hands, his mouth tight. She looked away and nodded. He sighed. "Probably just sick, maybe. Have you thought about going to work? Did you want to talk to the doctor?" She shook her head and he sighed again. He held the cage up to his face.

"You should keep it," he said. "It looks cool. Like art or something. You like art, right?"

"Yeah," she said as he placed the container back on her windowsill. "I used to doodle, I guess."

He reached up and scratched behind her ear like she was a dog. That night she still thought she heard the scratch of the crab's feet on the plastic, but every time she sat up it was still as ever. She touched her hands to the container and tilted it to the side. It slid across and ticked against the wall. She set it back down. Tomorrow she would go out, she thought. If only for an hour or two.

When he called the next day, he told her he'd be over soon to check on her. She waited, but he got held up somehow. She put her pillow over her head. It smelled like stale him. Through the padding she could still hear the clicking, but she knew the crab was dead. She put her hands to her stomach.

"Is it too dark out now to take a walk?" she asked. She sat up and opened the cage. She touched her finger to the claw. Ran it along the serrated edge, but it wasn't sharp enough to cut. In fact, she could hardly feel it at all. She took the container in both hands and shook it. The crab bounced around the bottom. A leg snapped off. She set it back down and pulled her blankets over her head. She sat there until she slipped into unconsciousness. She kept resurfacing. She thought she could feel something scratching against her thigh, her arm, the curve of her eyelid.

The next day she couldn't find the missing leg. He stood

in her doorway watching her crawl around on all fours searching her floor. She tore off her sheets. She flipped her mattress.

"It has to be here somewhere," she said. She looked up at him, glaring. "Why don't you help?"

"You've been acting a little weird, babe," he said, scratching his fingers against his five o' clock shadow. "Everything alright?"

She watched her hands spider through the carpet. In the dim light they looked grey. Lined. She pinched her fingers closed and pulled carpet fibers apart. Her stomach felt like it was unspooling.

"This doesn't seem normal. Do you want me to call the doctor?"

"No," she said, but her tongue twisted in her mouth. She heaved twice. Bile rose in her throat. Something sharp was lodging itself just below her tonsils.

She could hear him calling her. She spat up clear stomach acid. The crab's leg.

"What did you do? Oh god." He stepped back and covered his mouth. "Are you trying to get back at me? We talked about this. This isn't normal behavior. It isn't responsible. You couldn't even keep a crab alive. Do you see what I mean?"

She rolled on the floor and climbed onto her bed. She took the container in her hands, and chucked it at him. It fell short and the crab tumbled out onto the floor.

"I'm going to go," he said. "I'll come back tomorrow to check on you. Look, maybe we should look into finding help. Grief counseling." He stepped in and reached for the crab.

"Don't," she said. "Let me keep it. At least I can keep this."

He rubbed his eyes. "Fine. I can't fight about this tonight." He turned and shut the door. She laid on the floor and let her hair fall over her face. Through the weave she could see the crook of the crab's legs uncurling and sinking to the floor.

When she woke up the next day the puddle had dried, and the crab was gone. Her lips were sore. He was knocking.

"It's unlocked," she said. He opened the door and looked down at her. She stretched out and placed her hands against her stomach and smiled at him through half-closed eyes.

"Are you feeling better?" He asked.
Inside her she felt the tiny flutter. Like something was growing. Like something was breathing.

"Babe?" He said. "I don't think this is working. I know I said we could get through this, but you aren't even trying."
She placed a finger against her lips and shook her head. She motioned for him to come close. "Listen," she said, pointing to her stomach. She closed her eyes and heard the small clack of feet. The scratching.

"Listen." She said. "I can hear him kick.

Clown Town

Neither of us were happy with the neighborhood to begin with, but we were feeling cheap enough to settle for anything. The neighbors were the nice enough, I thought, even if they seemed a little fake and their smiles—well, they made me uneasy. And they drove you absolutely nuts. But they were the least of our many worries. The pastel striped houses, the smell of popcorn, the way the grass felt like candy corn, none of it was especially pleasant to us. Especially at that time in our life. Sometimes I wonder if that's what all tragedies really boil down to—the timing.

But in the end, what broke you was the balloons. They were over the top, I'll admit it. And if they were there when we were looking at the house, I doubt we would have ended up where we are now. But that's the thing about bad weather—no matter what meteorologists tell us, we can never really tell when it's going to roll in.

It was about three weeks after we moved in, if I remember correctly. Mid-afternoon. All day the wind had been threatening to be vicious. We were unloading groceries from the car when you saw the shadow crawling across the street. I came out to find you standing in the yard, bag clutched to your chest like an infant.

In the sky, they were already rising—a plague of balloons. Candy colored. Like a pop video let loose to flood the real world. It took them minutes to blanket the sky and block out the sun. All the light came down filtered in technicolor. It played on your face in a way that made me nauseous.

"What's going on," you asked.

"Maybe there's a party," I said, shrugging.

There was a cackle from the sidewalk. A little girl was peddling her trike down the street and had stopped to listen to us. We were a spectacle, I guess.

"You two are new, huh?" The girl said. I nodded and she sucked her teeth. Something about her seemed older than it should, but she was so small I don't think she could've been more than five. It must've been the pancake makeup. Or the way the balloon light played against the color of her face. She was in a patch of blue and it was positively corpse like, wasn't it? But that can't explain the two-packs-a-day voice she had, I guess. "It's the rainy season," she said. "You might want to buy some galoshes. It gets pretty bad."

"Okay." I said. "Thanks."

"No problem, doll." She peddled away, and you turned towards me, a yellow patch of light gliding across your eyes and over your mouth. I wanted to crack a joke. Maybe something about jaundice. Or the Simpsons. I was almost ready to, but then the paint started to fall. First just little splatters, then in long streaks.

 We gave up on the groceries and ran inside.

That whole season was terrible. Everything became an abstraction.

"I hate modern art," you told me. "It gives me a headache."

The helium had set in by then, and your voice was all Mickey Mouse. I laughed at you. What else could I do?

I was laughing at everything, then. Great big guffaws that made my rib cage ache. But it was all so funny.

The balloons. The paint spackled streets. The way you'd come in covered head to toe in color, and how it stained our bathtub mud black when you washed it off. The little girl and her pancake makeup. How the taste of the air made my throat close. The sweetness of our helium voices hiding their little barbs.

Cartoon arguments between muppets—who could even understand what they're going on about? All it is is noise. The season
wore on for months. Till all I ever did was laugh. Till it got so
bad that I couldn't breathe. Till it got so bad you just stopped
talking. Even then I kept laughing.
Even when I woke up and found the tracks of your suitcase
trailing off in the drying paint, I was laughing. Stood there
laughing until the little girl peddled past on her trike and
stopped to watch.
"Is it drying up?" I asked her, casting my eyes up to the balloon
spackled sky.
She looked from me to the sky. "Don't know. Could just be the
eye, I think. We'll have to wait and see."
I'm still waiting. I'm still laughing. There isn't much else I can
do.

THE DAUGHTER OF THE LAST AMERICAN COWBOY

The night she first fucks four different men within a span of six hours, her father dies and the crow shows up. That's not the order it all happened in. It would be more accurate to say that her father died, and the crow showed up, and then she fucked four different men. It is important to be accurate. It's also important to note it was in the past, but also, it is always happening for her.

She has trouble, sometimes, staying accurate, keeping track of time. She has to write it all down.

The crow rapped on her door, and she roused herself from the bed where she spends the majority of her time. She spent the majority of her life replaying scenes from before on the back of her eyelids and wondering what if at critical junctions. What if I had not said this, what if I had done this, what if the tilt of my head was wrong, the lilt in my voice.

She has done this since she started living alone; she has only lived alone for a short time. But by the time the crow shows up and her father dies and she begins fucking the men one after another, she does live alone. Her fiancé had left her two weeks before.

He was not her fiancé. He said he was going to be with her forever. But he was not her fiancé. He left her. He had never been her fiancé, but he had promised. She is alone now, when the crow knocks, with no longer even a not-fiancé to her name.

Your father is dead, the crow says when she opens the door. She, of course, does not see him at first. She is looking at the level where her not-fiancé's eyes would be, but they are not there. Instead, it is the crow with a baggie of powdered ashes resting between his two hooked feet.

Sometimes when she is laying in bed playing her what ifs she imagines what if her blood were made of flower petals. She imagines what if she split her wrists open and deluge of petals flooded her apartment, slipped out under the cracks of her door and filled the streets and she finally left the world with something beautiful. This, she tells herself, is the only desire she has left in life.

She thinks she is a Buddhist. She has no desire to live. She thinks this is being desireless. She thinks this is Buddhism.

What if she wonders and she pictures her not-fiancé's eyes behind her eyelids and presses her thumb against the pulse of her wrist.

The crow is so large that she could not cover its body with both of her hands, and she knows this because she picked it up and thought about throttling it when it told her your father is dead and you must bring the ashes to rest.

There is a bar where he played his music and he sang

his songs and you must bring him there, the crow said with her fingers distressing the feathers of his neck.

She had left him in the kitchen, but he had followed and knocked on her bedroom door until she could not wonder what if, what if, what if.

This is not a story, she tells him.

Not yet, the crow says.

She was the youngest of her father's children. Her father had many children. He fathered many children. He left them all when they were young. Except for her, he was too old to keep leaving when she was young. So instead, she left him.

He had been dying all her life. He never actually died. He is dead now.

He would sit in the dim of his bedroom and call her in to listen to his death rattle. Find someone, he would tell her, and don't fight them so, find someone and don't fight with them the way your mother fought me, find someone and you be good and don't want so much from them. Women were always fighting me. Women were always wanting too much. Women were always wondering why I left. I don't like fighting women. I don't like when people want too much of me. You be good, you don't fight, you don't want.

She didn't want to displease her father, and so rather than fight and expect, she left.

Was she not good enough, she wondered when her not-fiancé left, did she fight too much, did she want too much? She doesn't want much or fight much of anyone anymore, and she does not want her father's ashes. She does not want to bring them to rest.

They're yours, the crow says, regardless. You're the only child with nothing and no one else to be beholden to; you're the last; the one he stayed with and the one who left; he is owed and you are the one owing.

She releases the crow and takes the bag of ashes. She licked her thumb and pressed it to her forehead, anointing herself.

What are you doing, the crow asks.

A curse, she replies.

What if she were loved, she wonders, often. What if she were a soft thing to be cared for, she wonders. She had very seldom been soft when she was young, save for with her mother, who taught her to fight and want and leave, and then died before her father. That was not the order it was supposed to happen in, but it did. She had been a hard girl for everyone else other than her mother. Until her father began to rattle and rattle and rattle.

Without a mother, she began to be so lonely. She had wanted love. She had tried for love with her not-fiancé, but it hadn't come out right in the end. And now she was here, alone in the apartment, no mother, no father, no fiancé, or even not-fiancé, no love.

She was no one. She was not even no one. She wasn't even a Buddhist.

She had a desire.

My father wanted me so badly to find love, she tells the crow. I'll not sleep nor rest until I have it. And neither shall he. She pulls her thumb off of her forehead and there in the middle is a smudge of ash shaped like a perfect tear drop.

Your father wanted to be laid to rest where he wanted to be laid to rest, the crow says.

She walks out of the room to retrieve her phone without a reply.

Her father was not a cowboy. He just roamed a lot. He played jazz in dive bars. He took a lot of women. Herded them like cattle. He called himself a cowboy. He was a cowboy.

How does anyone become anyone, she wondered often to herself. Who am I to others? Who am I at all?

Your generation is nothing, her father said. We were the last greats. All you do now is live inside those screens. Nothing is real anymore. I'm the last of what is real, her father said. I saw stars, I traveled the country, I loved women, so many women. It was real, he insisted. I didn't sit in a cell of a room starting at made-up lights and color.

She was the daughter of a cowboy. She was not. She was no one.

What if there are flowers in my veins, she wonders, cradling her wrist of one hand in the other, the ash-smeared thumb pressed against her vein. In her cradled hand, she holds her phone, where she cycles through app after app, wondering what if someone could love me and I could be someone to someone?

What if I was something beautiful, what if I was something at all?

Of course, she didn't start with the apps. She had messaged her not-fiancé the way she sometimes did when she thought she had finally found the correct what if. He never messaged back, of course. She was never actually right about her what ifs.

No one has an obligation to anyone, her not-fiancé was fond of saying before he left, but still she tried. She waited, after she sent the message: My father has just died.

She saw that he read it. She saw the minutes go by after. Those minutes turn into hours. She wondered what if. What if he was with someone else? What if he was coming to her now? What if he had ever real loved her? What if?

What if no one had an obligation to anyone? What if she was no one's obligation?

And so, she turned to strangers.

Her father had been from the South, her mother and her from the North. Her father had traveled searching out women to love and leave. It is because you're from here, he told her once, that you and your mother's blood is so cold, that you are such hard people to love. You should have been born in the South. You should be warm if you're going to be loved.

When she left she went South, but no matter how far she traveled she still stayed cold.

What if I let my blood out to the sun, she wondered, would it bloom in the open air into something sweeter? What if I traveled farther—would I find somewhere to take root?

She did not have to travel to find men, however. She did not have to leave her house. They would come to her. One by one, they would come. Men were incredibly easy to find—and with them, what if love?

The first was over within thirty minutes of her first message. They sat at her small dining room table, and he, polite, did not ask about the crow and the ashes perched on top of her fridge, or the tear drop of ash on her forehead, or the red rim around her eyes. She tried being sweet, she tried not wanting too much, as he laid her down not even on her bed but the couch and took her, and while he did she risked asking him—tell me you love me—and he said it and he came in her and then he laughed and said that was wild, and great, but they probably should do it again.

That was some fucked up shit, he said, placing his hand on her forehead and his thumb on her ash to push her face backwards so she could see his face, and his laugh and his gleaming teeth. You're a fucked-up chick. It was fun.

And he left once it was understood he wasn't coming back.

It didn't matter, she tells herself, as on the screen there are other messages and other men waiting. When the second man comes over, she plays sweetness all over again, but this time does not make the mistake of asking for love.

There are enough of them that she has to keep track by writing them down and so she gives them names that are functions because too many of their names are the same. Names should be functions, she thinks, names should tell us who we are. She does not think any of them really remember her name, none of them say it—they call her kitten, or sweetheart, or babydoll, or bitch or whore or slut depending on what flavors they like, and less about who she is. She is more honest with the names she gives them; The Metal-head, the Divorcee, the Absentee Father, the Desperate Goth, the Damaged, the Emotionally Unavailable Musician, the Empty-Headed Himbo, the Faux-Spiritualist, the Hurtful One, the Hurting One, the Simple One, the Dead-End, the Dead Heart, the Choker, the Clinger, Mr. Two-Seconds, Mr. No-Seconds, Listless, Loveless, Little Hands, Little Feet, Little Hope, Missing Teeth, Missing Mom, the Comedian, the Heckler, the Married Bank Manager—she kept at first a diary of them on her own, but it seemed pointless writing about them to no one. It seemed like something no one would do, no one would care about.

What if, she thought between their visits, wide-eyed and reapplying the ash to her forehead, what if someone knew what I was doing—what if anyone cared?

And so she began to send her diary entries to her not-fiancé.

Are you a good person, the crow asks her, watching her type. To strangers, to her not-fiancé, to strangers, to not-fiancé, on and on and on.

I'm free after nine. When he came to me the first time, when he came inside of me the first time, he accidently called me by someone else's name. He's divorced—what if it was his wife's? What if we were divorced, what if we had married, would this feel any different? What if you felt anything at all? I could meet you here or there's a coffee shop down the road—I'm fine with meeting alone—Do you remember our first date? What if we could go back—You should bring the liquor this time, I'm out—What if we did things differently—It doesn't matter to me, we don't have to see each other anymore if you don't want— what if I had been the one who didn't care? Would you want me then? Do you want me, baby? I'm free tonight. One of them has my father's name, and he reminds me of you. Of the two of you. He plays music, like my father. He doesn't seem to care a lick about me. Like you. Like the both of you. I'll let you do what ever you want. Please. Come by whenever. I'm free all night. Please.

What if I'm not a person at all, she asks the crow.

It's been three days and the curse holds strong. She doesn't sleep, and her father's ashes sit nestled between the crow's hooked feet as he watches between his slow blinks.

Everything is always happening for her at once; it feels like nothing has ever really happened at all. Here is something that she is always living in:

Her not-fiancé is holding her in a lake and she has her legs wrapped around his waist. He is inside of her, with his teeth against her chin and she is murmuring as softly as the waves lap, and he whispers into her skin that she is his and he is hers and this is forever, they are waking up in a shared bed and he brings her a mug of hot coffee and they sit among the rumpled sheets speaking in half-waking dreams and body parts, he is bandaging her skinned palm and when it is done he puts the bandaged wound to his lips and he promises he loves her, they are sitting on a porch together during a thunderstorm and when there is a crack of light across the sky and she jumps, he laughs and bids her to come to his lap calling her and soothing her with baby baby baby, and she feels safe and small and cared for and she knows that this is it, this is home, when she sees him outside the bar, hand on another woman's waist, eyes full of another woman's eyes, she splits her wrist open and out pour petals, petals, petals, so he can see the love, all the love she had for him, pouring out into the street, see that she was beautiful, see that he never should have left, that he never should leave— he was always leaving—him, in the doorframe, his back towards her more familiar than the feeling of his hands—if he would turn and look and see her—see inside her something beauti- ful—he had come to her once, his shoulders sagged and ran his hands over his face—I love you, I've decided to love you, he'd said, he'd said, he had promised–

–all of these things play simultaneously in her head at all times, somewhere in the back, along with a long list of what ifs. The moments, the list, they add upon each other. Grow longer. She is never fully anywhere; everything is always happening for her all at once, nothing is ever happening for her really.

Now, or sometime, she was sitting on the porch with the Emo- tionally Unavailable Musician. She has been awake six days, or maybe three weeks, or maybe she is sleeping right now. They are smoking cigarettes, and she is in his lap and there is rain, but no thunder and she wonders what if there were thunder, would she jump and would he sooth her would he call her baby baby baby, would she be soothed? Would it feel like a home? What if he could love me. *I think he could love me,* she tells her not-fiancé, I *want him to love me, I want to love him, I want us* *to be in love the way we never really were. Did it even happen? If you never really did—did it even—*she wants to tell him that she loves him tonight. The crow sits on the telephone wire with the bag of her fathers ashes in clamped tight against the downpour in his beak.

You're my favorite, she says into his neck and he groans.

The thing about you, he says, is that I just keep feeling this hesitation. I can't put my finger on it.

He pulls her hand off of his shoulder, her wrist throbbing with blood beneath his thumb. He is saying something to her. But she is wondering—

What if my veins are filled with flowers, what if there is something beautiful inside of me—if I let someone inside of me why don't they see it—she is seeing her not-fiancé's back in the framed by the doorway, she is seeing him with his mouth on another mouth she is pressing down on her own wrist and then he is taking her home.

What if you had loved me she types, *what if you had loved me, what if I had been beautiful what if—*

She sits upright in her bed and watches her phone screen while the crow sits on her lamp and watches her. She is trailing her thumb through her father's ashes. The messages are trailing in slower and slower. Her breath: slower and slower; her heart; slower and slower. The works are gummed up, she thinks, reapplying her curse.

When she pulls the thumb off her forehead and brushes it on her jeans, she asks the bird: will I get a crow when I die?

Your father created, the crow said. People remember him. People loved him. So he deserves to be put to rest.

My father was a liar, she says. He was no cowboy, no great, my father wasn't real.

And yet I'm still here, and he still deserves to be put to rest, and to hang among the stars, the crow says. Maybe some lies are realer than reality.

Where is it he wants to go, she asks, dislodging a stubborn bit of her father from beneath her fingernail with her teeth. Not that I'm going to now, but I may as well know.

The bar he played his first gig at, says the crow. Where he met many women who loved him and who he loved. Your mother not among them.

Did he put my mother to rest, she asks.

It's different for men, you know, the crow says. I will give you that. Things are different for men. Your women folk, you let people in so easily. You let yourselves be consumed too easily. You hope too much for a home. A home in a person. And so, you make yourselves homes for people. You know women were designated mourners, in the old times, it was women's jobs to mourn men, to put them to rest.

Will I be put to rest, she asks, returning to the start.

It's different, the crow says.

Her phone dings.

Some tell her its over, some just disappear. There were too many to keep track of at first, and some she's never sure are truly gone. The hours have become too many to keep track of. The goodbyes. She sends a message to Emotionally Unavailable Musician, to Activist Lawyer, to Single, Inattentive Father, and she can't place who has disappeared and who has not. Married Banker replies and when he touches her it feels like she is covered in slimy things; his fingers are worms inside her and his mouth feels like a shell pressing against hers and letting loose a fat, writing mollusk inside of her mouth.

I love you, she says, wriggling underneath him, her eyes bloodshot and her mouth dry with exhaustion. I love you, I love you, I love you.

Sure baby, he says, fumbling with his belt, I love you, too.

And when she closes her eyes, she pictures her mother as his wife and she pukes just a little, and it spills out all over her own neck and his bloated chest.

He fumbles backward, shouting, and she thinks if he has children he should be used to this, but she doesn't remember if he does or doesn't. Still she reaches out with both her hands like a little girl and begs.

Please, help, please?

But he is out the door before she can even rise off the pillows. On the lamp the crow coos softly and begins to clean its own wings.

What if she thinks and begins to cry, running her hands over her face and smearing the tears and her vomit all together.

In the bath, she messages her not-fiancé. Tonight the man with my father's name is playing a show. Last night he told me he wanted me there. That he wanted me. He told me he wanted me the way you said you wanted me only with him there is no hesitation. He said he never feels any hesitation.

The crow watches as she shaves her legs, sitting on the bathroom counter with her father's ashes under his wing.

What's the name of the place, she asks the crow. Her eyes have started drifting when they are open. More red than white, more dry than wet. How long can a human body, cursed or otherwise, last without sleep?

The Wilted Rose, the crow says, thirty minutes from here.

That's it, she says back and lays back in the water, that's where the man who loves me is playing tonight. She tells her not-fiancé so.

What if she types you showed up there? That you knew now that someone loved me how much you had loved me, how much you miss me, how much you want me back—you could come, what if you come?

After it's sent she dunks her head in the water, emerges, and dries off. Once dried, she puts on her best dress, lines her tired eyes and shades them, colors in her cracked lips, and reapplies her father's ashes to her forehead.

She is no one, she is alone, she is loved, she is waiting for her love outside of the Wilted Rose. Inside there is a man who loves her. He is a musician with her father's name. A bag of ashes sits heavy in her hands. It is no one. It is her father. The last great American Cowboy.

The crow sits on the telephone wire and watches her hover near the bar door. There is music beyond it, yes, there are bodies moving.

She places her hand on the door and feels its vibrations through her fingertips up her arm. Through her veins. There is something there; something growing, something humming.

What if I open myself up she wonders, will roses grow? My father saw the stars, and roamed, and played his songs and was the last American cowboy, he was a great man who hung the stars, and I am his daughter, full of flowers. She brings the bag to her chest and holds it in one hand, her wrist with the other, her thumb pressed against the thrumming in her veins. I am loved and desired and my father is watching my wedding from the stars.

What are you doing, the crow asks from the telephone wire.

Going to my wedding party, she says, and she steps into the bar.

She had wanted to dance; brides should dance. No body wanted to dance with her; she was no bride. Each person she went to with open arms recoiled. Each hand she grabbed hold of withdrew. They pushed her from person to person, and in her tired eyes the lights blurred and smeared, and the voices rose into and angry hum, and try as she might to keep her father's ashes grasped tight in her hand, they spilled out here, there and everywhere until the bag was nearly empty and then she was spun out the door with the remains of his remains to land on the cement.

The rest of her father scattered among broken bottles and cigarette butts. She scrambled to her knees and clutched here and there for them but they were gone. In her hands, there was nothing left but scraps of trash and broken glass. Her phone dinged. The screen lit up. A message from her not-fiancé. What if she wonders, and her hands are trembling. He'll come, and he will lift her up and he will take her home, she will tell him where she is and—

I'm happy you're happy finally, the message reads, *so let me go. You were right all along, you know. I never really did love you. It was just something I'd said because I thought you needed to hear it. I'm glad you're loved now. Please leave me alone.*

Some lies are realer than reality, she accuses the crow.

It's different for men, the crow admits. I never lied about that.

He looks at her one last time as she takes the glass in her hands, and then with one low coo, he takes to flight and leaves her truly alone.

What if, she thinks, my father is up there among the stars, what if my blood is full of flowers, what if he is really coming, someone to love me, what if something inside me is beautiful—

All it takes is a little pressure and pull, all it takes is a two tears, and she feels a glorious warmth all down her wrist. What if she thinks, closing her eyes and picturing vines and beautiful buds of all colors stretching out in every direction, trailing off to find them all—all the men who never loved her— to lead them with their perfume and their beauty back to her, so that they might finally see—so that she might finally be loved—

But when she opens her eyes, there are no stars in the sky, nor birds coming to put her to rest, not men with their arms open and their voices softly soothing her with baby, baby, baby, and her blood, her blood that's pouring out, well, it's nothing more than that.

Little Things

It started raining on Monday, and it didn't stop. By Wednesday the streets were three feet deep in water, and the mayor had shut the city down. The sewers had flooded. There was literal shit filling the streets. You hated being inside with me, and hated even more that I had stuffed towels under the doors to keep the water and the smell of sewer out. You wanted to let it all in. Instead you laid by the window staring out at the rain as it fell, at the current of water sloshing downhill into the bottom of the cul-de-sac.

"Honey," I said on Friday, after two days of silence. "The news is on."

"My mother always said I was a fish. We were both fish, me and her. Water signs." Your skin looked waxy and grey by the window, like you were becoming one of the storm clouds you were watching.

"That's nice," I said, turning the volume down on the television.

"Let's play a game," you said. "Tell me thirty things I've never heard you say. Thirty secrets."

"I don't feel like playing right now," I said. You lapsed back into sullenness, your forehead pressed against the window. Like you were a child moping.

Saturday the power was out. I spent the morning rearranging our house. It had grown cluttered with too many years. The little things we'd taken a liking too, taken home, and stuffed on shelves to be forgotten. Shot glasses from Mexico. Dutch girl figurines stooping to kiss one another. A hand-carved top from our visit to Amish Country. There were little bits of dust on it all, and I spent hours trying to wipe them clean as the rain kept going, going, going. But the dirt in the corners or minute crevices was stubborn. The pictures we had framed of us from back when we first met were especially bad. Eventually I gave up, and sat on the couch with my back to it all, eyes on the blank T.V. In the afternoon you woke up, and told me that you always knew I never really wanted to get married, and that could count as my number one.

"That's not true," I told you. You just shrugged and went on looking out the windows. I wrung out the towels in the bathroom sink, and when I came back water had already slunk through the crack in the door. You were standing in it barefoot. You lifted your arms out to me, and tried to smile as it trickled between your toes.

"It's not so bad, is it?" you asked. But it smelled horrible.

"I hate it when you act like a kid," I told you.

"That's number two," you said, sitting down in the puddle, your back against the door. I let the towel drop and walked away. By that point the power was out and the water outside reached halfway up the windows. All we had left was spaghetti. I cooked it on a small kerosene stove we bought back when you insisted we go camping. I hovered over the pot, letting the steam wash away the stench of the sewer. I heard you in the next room, splashing.

"This has got to end." Saturday night bled into Sunday morning and the rain kept falling. "This has got to end." Neither of us slept. I kept whispering to myself. "This has got to end." The water was to your ankles. I was laying on the couch. I heard your steps sloshing towards me. You bent over me. Your fingers brushed my lips, wet. I wanted to recoil. I thought of E.coli and other sewer sicknesses. I wanted to grab you and shake you. I wanted to rub your face against the window. "This has got to end," is all I said.

Lightning cracked outside, and in its light I saw you nod, but if you spoke I couldn't hear it over the thunder. You turned away from me and went back to your window.

That's when it started to tumble out. All in one great long breath whispered to the shadow of your back. The thirty ways I didn't love you anymore.

Do you remember back when we first were getting to know each other? Do you remember how I used to always be the one to leave first? It drove you crazy, how easy it was for me to tear myself away from you. How easy it was for me to hang up the phone. But you never said anything about it. We were still trying to be agreeable, then. We were trying to stretch it out into a habit. Anything we didn't like, we didn't say.

The night we broke the habit, you told me that love took substance. It took a brokenness. It took shards of glass. You were drunk in a way I'd never seen you before. Afterwards, it happened often enough that I could predict the nights on a calendar. You were cross-eyed and blathering that first night. You took my hands in yours and held them up to my face. "They're so clean," you said with contempt. "They're so soft." The next morning we laughed about it. You were dressed in my clothes. You had puked on your own.

It took a brokenness, you had said.

After that night, you always talked like that when you got too drunk. Being broken. Your mother and her corpse. The string of bad lovers you wore like a necklace. I would just listen until you'd pass out, tear-streaked cheeks pressed to the floor. You'd never sleep in bed with me those nights. So I'd sit on the bed alone, watching, and listening, and waiting for you to stop. At the end you always looked at me, tongue poking out between your teeth, eyes narrowed. Like there was something I wasn't giving you. I think you wanted me to say it. That you were fucked up. That I didn't love you. Or maybe you just wanted me to climb down onto the floor with you.

I'm sorry I never figured out which.

Sometime between dawn and noon, I fell asleep. When I woke up the water had flooded in. It was lapping my shoulders as I lay on the couch. I got to my feet to stand on top the cushions. The water had dribbled into my shoes and soaked the back of my shirt. I saw you standing in the doorway. You had opened our front door, and let it all in. You were holding your arms out to the sky.

"It's not so bad," you said.

"Close the door."

You shook your head, and pushed against the current washing in. All around me the little knick knacks of our life together bobbed in the waves. A photo of us drifted by, the paper dissolving under a thin layer of murky brown water. I watched it sink as a fresh wave rolled in. When I looked up you were outside. You were doing the breaststroke. You were swimming to the street. The current was carrying you downhill. And then you weren't you. You were scaled, and small, leaping, and then gone. A salmon doing what salmons do.

The next day the rain slowed to a drizzle. The house emptied. When the water poured out it sucked all of our stuff

with it. A trail of the small artifacts of our life leading over the threshold and down the hill. I didn't get up to shut the door. I didn't clean the mess. I stayed shivering on the couch, waiting for you to follow them home. I recounted all the things I'd told you, repeating the last one, over and over. The one you'd made into a lie when you stepped outside into the rain.
When you left me first.

Love Breaks My Bones, and I Laugh

Sometimes when I am passing by windows at night, I will catch the faintest outline of a person's silhouette behind the glass and the curtains, and I'll slow my walk. That's not true, actually. Sometimes I have a problem with lying. It isn't good to be too honest too quickly, I've learned that. I will stop, completely, you know. My right foot, a paper weight. Their face, featureless behind the linen.

There is something in the lines of the human body, something potent and changeable, something beautiful and terrifying, there is something in the human body like a great claw when you watch it alone, when it is alone, when it is terrified of being alone. Anyway.

I have a bad habit of standing there and watching the silhouettes like they are canaries beneath a great cloth sack that might start singing if I wait. That might start singing if I can tear away the lined linen between us.

In those moments I do have a feeling. I can't help that kind of feeling, you know, and I wonder where is it we keep ourselves. Is it in the meat and the bone, or is it in the brain, or is it in the face, or in the words we speak to one another, the stories we tell and what we say? Where are we in all of ourselves? Sometimes its true I worry I am using up all my words, and that the next person I speak to will be the last, and who will I be then? What kind of shadow?

I have been worried, you know that. I know that you don't like my worry. I have known this longer than you can even imagine, and yet, there is a feeling. There is a feeling, you can't deny that can you? Even if you can't know it all, top to bottom. Anyway.

There's a story about a girl I knew once that needs telling. That I need to tell you. Because I want you to be more than that. For us to be more than apparitions to one another passing behind a curtain. I have wanted this for a very long time, perhaps longer than one should.

One day this girl wakes up in bed. She isn't alone in the bed. She has been alone before this. She has been in and out of loneliness, and each entrance and exit feels like a pollution. There is something in her guts, she thinks, some great writhing thing. A feeling she feels sometimes, it's true, you know. But for the time being she has stopped being alone. In the bed with her is a man. For our purposes, lets call him Mr. Loverman, though of course this is not his name. But sometimes this is more true, to refer to a person as their function, their relation to you, or rather, maybe in her case, what she is wishing his function and his relation to her to be, though it is not yet who he is and what he is doing, and so therefore may not be that true at all. Anyway, that's what we'll call him for now.

She wakes with her face pressed against his breast and a thin layer of sweat bubbling between their skin trying to adhere them together, and what a wonderful way to wake, she thinks, and how terrifying and hopeful the thought of adhering. She is laying there thinking and feeling these things when she feels something like the writhing she has kept in her guts through the entrances and the exits and the long decades, all three adding up their hurts. Only it is outside of her. It is tickling her thighs and the hip that lays against the bed, and running along the length of her leg. She pulls back the blanket and sees a puddle of white collected between their nude groins. Writhing and pulsing and searching across their skin.

Maggots, of course. Freshly birthed.

You wake in the morning and wash your face in the mirror and do you look at it a beat too long? I wonder, you know. I want to know. You walk to work, and you take everything at a leisured pace. You have such a confident step, so steady and never lagging or rushing or pausing as if you are in the grip of something eldritch and unknowable. I envy that, and maybe that is what started it all was envy, but I'm not quite sure. Something like envy, something like desire. There is a feeling, you know. Can you at least not deny me that much?

And so, you move through the day. You move through day after day. You must know you too, are aging. You must know, for you too, doors close, and paths overgrow, and soon, very soon, who knows what will be left, but you don't walk that way or seem to be searching for anything. Is that true? Am I seeing you clearly?

Someone once told me the wisdom to quit is all we have, and I hated that. Because its not true. I have never even had that.

Anyway, she wakes to maggots, that morning long ago. And she goes to scoop them out of her bed before Mr. Loverman wakes and sees what a monstrous birth has occurred between them. She is scooping them up in her bare hands and standing to go and throw the lot of them in her toiler when one winds its way up through the crevice of her fingers and she sees it there, bloated and pure white, and looking like at any moment something might bloom from its tip.

And she stalled—foot a paper weight, face slack, and wondered. What kind of mother was she?

And he woke, and he screamed and instead of throwing them away she hid her handful of maggots behind her back, but it was too late, he had already seen.

#

The city grows, the plants recede, and no one, not a single soul, loves the sight of a maggot even though they are often the last scrap of nature we have left. Even though they are just a thing, trying to live, trying to love, like all other things. All the birds are out of the sky and all that rises above the horizon now is concrete and flies. Filthy air, smokestacks, and curses. All identical and featureless, all casting everything behind a shade.

I want to see a bluebird, its true.

Nobody looks at maggots. Nobody looks at flies. Nobody.

I want someone to look at me like I am the last bluebird, that is truer.

Above all I want that person to be you, but I am told that is just a feeling.

He leaves, after that, of course. Who wouldn't leave, seeing something like that? Nobody likes to look at maggots, and he can't unsee the place they once took up in her palm. She stays mostly laid down afterwards, the maggots in a cup by her bed she dribbles ash and garbage into with a limp hand. Or she brings them with her when she sits in front of her computer and cycles between digital counselors. She has always needed counseling. She can't trust the feeling; the great claw in her belly; the dark cast of her thoughts like a silhouette behind linen. She fluctuates, a problem she has always had. She speaks to a psychic online. She speaks to therapist. She asks them, where did he go; will he return; will he ever love me.

"I've pulled the lovers card, dear," says one psychic, "rest assured."

"You need to focus on yourself. You need to give yourself love to grow," says the therapist.

But she knows so little of love, how is she supposed to do that? She has been given so little, she only has a little to give. She gives it to the maggots in trash and cigarette ash and the salt of her pitiful crying.

 The maggots grow; they don't need much love to, just a little. Just a little feeling, and maggots will grow.

As she lays there, wounds playing against the screens of her eyelids, they blossom into flies. They are grateful children; they have to be grateful. So seldom does anyone stay with a maggot until it blooms.

The flies come to rest on her body as she lays prone and she messages her counselors and she watches people move through out the world, just shadows behind the great white sheet of her curtains and the flies worry, the way grateful children do.

"Mother," they say, "what do you want?" they ask, because they love her despite being little, because they love her despite having so little love to give.

"I want to go back," she says. "I want to try again. Go back in time."

"Time can't be folded or changed, Mother," the flies say. "But you can."

"How?" she asks. And they show her.

Do you know yourself? If you close your eyes and search can you find a part of you hard and stable and protected like a nut in a shell? Do you know you? Do you want to?

Where are you, in all of this? I have been groping for you, for your feeling. I have wanted to know it. To take the core of you in my hands and put it to my mouth. To kiss it. To plant it inside myself. To let something be born from it; to let something grow. Not something like maggots, no. Something like a tree. A tree a bird might come to rest in. Anyway.

I have closed my eyes. I have looked for my own. But its just like when I am walking down the street. Whoever she is is behind a great linen sheet. Whoever she is is just a silhouette. I keep waiting for her to sing. But can we hear ourselves?

Do our selves exist, if there's no one else there for us to be for?

I am who I am and have need to be. Do you remember that? But of course you don't. It wasn't me you read that with; it was another girl. Another girl from sometime ago that you are already forgetting. But please, don't.

The flies swarm her. With their loving mouths they spit and dissolve the skin and flesh from her bones. They take her in until she is all skeleton, and then they take more until she is all guts, and then they take more until she is just a puddle, and something small in that puddle writhing and reaching, covered and muck and unknowable. In their guts, the flies churn her, they mix, they grind, they change. And then they spit her back out again, piece by piece by piece, only she is different. Her innards coiled in a new pattern, her bones aligned just slightly off from how they once were, her flesh stretched over it all like a fresh blanket. Her face is not the face she knew when she looks in the mirror.

Only the flies know who she once had been, and of course, her counselors who had never seen her in person.

"How do you earn love?" she asks them.

"The universe will open it up for you, it will crack it open like a shell. I see in the stars, this will happen for you very soon. I see in the stars, next Tuesday, you will find love," says the psychic.

"You shouldn't have to earn love," says the therapist. "Love isn't something that's earned. You have a right to be loved. The right person will love you."

She shuts down the computer and she waits until Tuesday. Then she makes up her new face, and combs out her new hair the way she knows he likes it, and she goes and finds Mr. Loverman where he often is. And she smiles, when they bump into each other. And she gives him a new name.

If I am going to believe in anything, it is going to be this: anything can change. Anything can be fixed. You just have to find the right combination. Of feeling. Of timing. Of words. But I feel I am running out of words, though. Running out of combinations. This is likely the last time. These are likely the last words. Anyway.

I can see you know, now, where this is going. I know your face so well. So much better than my own. Mine is like a stranger to me, its expressions completely different from the expressions I feel on the inside. I know you know now, the story I am telling. There's a feeling there, in your face. Terror, yes. I can see it. But please, listen anyway. Because this is my last story. This is my last self.

After that Tuesday, there is good between them, yes for a little, there is sweetness the way there had once been sweetness, there is growing the way there once had been growing. She never takes him home, of course, so he cannot see who she once was, and so he cannot see her flies. And yes it drives him wild, and that wildness feeds the growing, the sweetness. And so she learns withholding. She learns not to be too honest too quickly.

"I see the tower," says her psychic, "darling, I see disaster."

"It's good to have boundaries," her therapist agrees.

And so, she draws them, and she withholds, and she is never too honest, she is never too open and eventually that wildness gives way to a collapse. Eventually, all things lead to collapse.

"How can I love you?" he says. "How can I when I don't even know you?"

But what has love ever had to do with knowing? She doesn't know. It always collapses before she can.

She goes back to her flies, who she has neglected. She goes back to her flies who are weak. The strongest of them drag themselves across her counters and lap up what remains there that they can. The weakest of them have died, and lay on their back, shriveled like raisins.

She gathers those that have survived in her palm, and lays herself down on her bed.

"Again," she says. They set their hungry mouths to her flesh.

Why would she do it?

Because of the feeling of course. Because inside of her there is a great claw, wanting, reaching, trying to hold on. Because there was a feeling.

A feeling like a panicked rabbit. A feeling like she was wrapped all up in linen and could not breath. A feeling like she was dissolving, always dissolving. A feeling like her eyes were closed and she was searching for something hard and stable within herself and coming back with only a puddle, damp and easily stirred, dissipating. Because there is a feeling, a feeling of reaching.

And when she had reached, hadn't everyone always pushed that searching claw away? Hadn't they'd always withdrawn, as if she was a gross and writing thing?

But once, there was Mr. Loverman, and he had swung her into his arms, yes. He had met that searching claw with his hand and he had pulled her close, and placed his mouth next to her ear, and had whispered something so sweet in her ear it was almost like love.

And all the feeling stopped, and instead she felt something new. An egg hatching to something feathered and beautiful among the smog and the silhouettes and the terrible, writhing things no one wants to see.

She goes back with her new fingers to the old keyboard and she asks her questions. What is love? When will love come? Will he love me? She wears the letters of the word of her keyboard with her typing. Blank spaces where once love stood.

"Maybe you need medication," the psychic says.

"Have you tried believing in a higher power? Have you tried manifesting? Have you ever tried to scream your need to the moon?" the therapist asks.

But the moon is hidden from her behind the clouds when she goes out, so instead she goes past his house and watches the shape of his body move behind the curtain between them and she aches, and there is a feeling, there is a great claw scratching her from within.

When he comes out and sees her she waves a hand and pretends to smile, and acts as if she has lost her contact, and he helps her search even though there is no contact, her eyes are perfect and new and wide as a baby's. She tells him a new story of self, and he smiles at her, and looks.

And she feels like that again; like the last blue jay come home to roost.

And it all begins again.

And it all begins again.

The first kiss; the hundredth. New words; a new story; a new face.

The feeling starts; the words fail; the feeling stops; the story ends.

She sits across him and listens to him describing an ex, a memory where she was worried. "She was always worried," he says, "and once she just shut down, outside of this house on the street, just looking at a window, just watching someone, and she began to cry. I didn't know how to handle feelings like that."

The memory lashes out and wraps itself around her and she is there again outside the window, him walking ahead of her, him leaving her behind, and she feels alone, and so isolated behind the glass, behind the linen. She feels herself, a bird carcass super glued to the spot by her own dissolving flesh.

"She probably," she says, swallowing the lump in her throat. "She probably just wanted to be held. She probably just needed love."

He shrugs. "I just didn't feel as much for her as she did for me."

"Do you—do you feel anything for me?" she asks, still trying to swallow the claw now climbing its way out of her throat.

There is a feeling. You have to give me at least that. There is a feeling.

She comes home, and he has deleted her new number, her new body has turned old. More flies dead. More words wasted. Another story ended.

"Please," she types.

"You're a neurotic," says the psychic. "No one can love a neurotic. You can't manipulate yourself into love."

"Throw some bones on the ground, see the word they spell, there is your answer," the therapist says.

She throws her bones on the bed. She lays with her last living flies.

"Again," she says, dreaming up another story. Another self.

"I love you," she whispers into his ear, and she hears silence echo back, and beneath the covers he pulls over himself as he turns away, he looks like nothing more than a vague shape, so far away.

#

But it is there—you have to admit, there is something there. If you would look. If you would let it bloom.

Please.

I don't want us to become just silhouettes.

Love Breaks My Bones, and I Laugh

REWRITES

At night he comes to me, weeping again. Hans Christian An-
dersen. You have just left. You are always leaving. I am trapped
in this moment, always. Hans coming, you going. My legs torn
open, and blood blotching the rumpled bedsheets like spilled
ink. Hans climbs into the bed with me, ungainly and with hands
as large as my face to hold me from behind. His hook nose rests
next to my ear, just a memory pretending to breath.

Let me tell you a story, I say.
      Let me tell you a story. It starts. Once upon a time.
      You sit across from me at a table, and our hands are a
hair's breadth away. This is the way a story should start. But it is
not where ours starts. It is just another part of the pattern. The
story starts with Hans.

In the morning, I lay limp in Hans' arms as he sits me at the
table. My hand in his hand, we take the pen. Sentences crawl
across the page, unfurling like ribbons. Scabs grow over my
legs. Hans tells me I will dance again.
      How will it feel? I ask.

Like blades. Like blades.

Neither of us have ever felt beautiful. We look to our words.

The pen has stained our fingertips.

A story starts with a hello. A hand rests next to a hand. A mouth next to a mouth. In the middle we breath together in the dark of a bedroom, and we listen to the tangible evidence of our bodies. A heartbeat, a stirring of the guts, I feel the flutter of your eyelashes against my forehead, the sweat pooling between our stomachs. Solid things; things not of Hans and ink. I hold my lips to your cheek with hope.

But Hans has been with me since the beginning and he watches from the corner, and as you turn over, I see him standing there over your shoulder, and when our eyes meet, of course, we know.

A story starts with hello and ends with goodbye. The middle only serves to carry you there.

As a child, I died and came back.

Hans had always loved children.

Hans had always waited in the corner, trying to make the children laugh.

Hans had always been lonely.

As a child, I had been lonely.

As a child, I died and came back. Clutching his coattails, dragging him with me into the dark forest of my heart.

We live there together, now. We have never been apart.

We both have always been alone.

Tell me a story, I say. I'll tell you a story.

In the evening when the sun has dropped the page is printed. Once upon a time. The story begins. Your name bleeds through the first page onto the next, onto the next. Hans watches as I spread the lipstick across my lips.

He loved a ballerina once. He loved a Grand-Duke. He loved, day in and day out. Hans, a great lover, was always spilling out of himself. He tells me the stories. Hands were never his to hold. Always a hair's breadth away. Hans, my sweet Hans. Do we love? I ask. He has only done so through letters. What does he know of tangible love and touch? He's never known anyone to return.

We are trying.

I leave him in the corner where he waits and walk back to our beginning.

A hand rests near a hand. We cross the space between and enter the middle. We lay beneath the watchful eye of Hans. It starts with hello. We sleep tangible arms in tangible arms, and in my dreams the mattress is a ship tossing on the waves. I am watching your back at your wedding day. Below, Hans waits with the knife laid across his lap.

We know where it is where I belong.

We know the ending.

We've wrote it enough.

Sometimes when someone dies, they are living on borrowed time. My sweet Hans, he is keeping me alive. Every tear adds a day to our trial. Every time there is a smile, we fade a little. The pain will keep us present, we say.

A knife is offered, a return is offered. Bleed the heart of your beloved; a heart for a heart; a stone tossed into the ocean; dissolution in place of desire.

We don't have a soul. A soul is earned through love, Hans tells me.

How badly we want love. How badly we want to go on existing.

Salvation for the soulless is destruction; salvation for the soulless is a palace of ice; a prick of glass in the heart of your eye; a narrative in the cold of night.

We want someone to see us dance on the knife's edge, and we want them to stay. To see that every step is pain on freshly minted legs. To swoop us up and carry us away.

You see; you leave; Hans comes to my bed and he holds me.

Three hundred years, and every tear, another day added. I'll never leave you, we say.

In the bed, we light fire to the pages and in it we see all the possibilities of love burning away. You and I, in a garden of tale-telling roses. You and I hanging off the back of a sled. You and I climbing through the knot of a tree; at the end of the tunnel there is a treasure waiting. You and I at the end of the aisle. We dance.

The endings never come out right. They are always in need of revision. In the end you always leave.

We warm our hands over the fire and watch the images dissolve into ash. When they have burned out completely, Hans feeds them to me.

We wake in the morning, bloodstained with ash mouths, and Hans puts me at the desk, his hook nose resting near my ear, the pen in our hands.

I am willing to help you, Hans says, but are you willing to suffer all this?

Let me tell you a story, I'll tell you a story.

My voice, long mute, spills onto the page.

We write and write again.

Couri Johnson is an author, editor, and educator living in New Orleans, LA. She is the author of the short story collection, *I'll Tell You a Love Story*, and the forthcoming novel-in-stories, *The Girl Who*. She writes contemporary fairy tales for the bitter and mentally unwell.

Pumpernickel House Puiblishing and its imprints, Black Annis Books and Half-Light Press, is a publishing house dedicated to expanding the conversation about the overlap between genre and liteary fiction. We aim to provide diverse authors outside of just academia to publication, promotion, and community/ workshop opportunities. For information about upcoming events, classes, books, or to submit, please visit: www.pumpernickelhousepublishing.com

Thank you to all who have already joined our community, sub-mitted, or attended our events. We'd be nothing without you!

9 798218 166960